Eccentric Orbits

An Anthology of Science Fiction Poetry

Volume 3

Edited by
Wendy Van Camp

Contents

FOREWORD:

As a speculative poet, I'm often asked why I choose this theme for my work. To me, there is no more worthy topic to write. From ancient times, poets have looked to the stars and the mythos for their inspiration. In contemporary times, we expand on this basic instinct to include travel to the stars, a look within the supernatural, or how the advances of technology will change our lives. Speculative fiction and poetry is the gateway of exploration of how humanity will tackle these new concepts. The function of speculative poetry is to engage the mind, to allow the poet to guide the reader to new horizons and inner understanding. Within this anthology, you will hear the voices of thirty-nine modern day speculative poets, many of whom are at the top of their field. Journey with these wordsmiths as their words surge from the pages of science fiction into the reality of our world.

Wendy Van Camp
Editor
Eccentric Orbits 3

The Gift of Spirit
by Deborah L. Kelly

I am moved to the edge
of the cosmos; an unseen
force beckons me forward with
the magic of pure thought.

>Something has enveloped
>>me in an energy capsule, complete
>>with enough to support my
>>mortal form: sustenance, gravity,
>>rest, as the heavens rush
>>past me upon this wondrous
>>journey through the vast reaches
>>of space.

Where is it taking me?
Who is the master behind the creation
of this magnificent craft, carrying
me gently, yet swiftly, to an unknown
destination?

>>*There is no feeling of motion,*
>>*no vibration nor sound.*

I am coming upon what looks
like an edge; but an edge to where?

>>*In a flash of the brightest light I have*
>>*ever seen, I walk the streets of what*
>>*my mind tells me is a dream; another*
>>*universe has opened before me, a*
>>*dimension of different sights and sounds.*

Bells upon mountain peaks, just ahead of me …
>light, pure light, as far ahead and around
>me as spirit eye sees, for I am no
>longer within my earthen body.

A gentle light being has placed hand upon my shoulder,
showing me just how much older our souls truly are.

*As glorious beings of light,
we have travelled multiple universes for eons;
we shall continue for eons more ... unto the light
of distant shores, spreading the gift of Spirit to all new worlds
we encounter.*

Sun-Like

by Jean-Paul L. Garnier

couple of times
in reach
this is it
kindling it was

house burned
dog dead
ashes to make clay

those stars never stopped
seemed like Hell, lots
the long times
all the black in-between

that old shovel dings against a rock sometimes
rattles the wrist in a bad way
in reach, so to say
building up a new house
all tinder ripe for fire
burning in the good way
all sun-like
and eternal for now

The Mystery
by Jack Massa

This Universe is a snail
Endlessly crawling the rim of a donut.
Or it could be a breath of air
Trapped in the lungs of a mermaid.

Certainly, it is a bottomless dark ocean
And the stars are its foam.
(Science tells us this much.)

But perhaps it is also a snowflake
Melting on the tongue of a bear,
Or the skin of an apple peeled
By the fingernail of a child.

Really, it is whatever you will.
Because Will is the stem of Desire.
And though I can begin to tell you everything,
Sadly--or not--I can tell you nothing.

The Shrike
by Justin Sloane

Vlad the Impaler
but with very pretty feathers

the shrike is really quite
the impressive bird

a flying impaler

-- Hello, my vicious little Rotrückenwürger!
What feathered friend
gets the Iron Maiden treatment on this fine medieval day? --

but for the nightmarishly thorny
ornithological disposition

it would probably be much more popular

with the tweed, tobacco pipe, and binocular set

who much prefer idyllic scenes of the birdly life

to the gore, the ghoulish castle-dungeon bloodfest

that shrikes like the best, at their lunchtime

Vlad the Impaler,
but with very pretty feathers

in Transylvania,
they really couldn't have done it much better

the winged impaler

-- Can a thorn bush
be considered technology? --

imagine if shrikes were the size

of Andean condors

with ten-foot wingspans and an appetite for humans

a flying impaler

swooping down at high speed
skewering dog walkers on the nearest branch

Beware the Shrike!

Danger of Shrike Attack!

signs posted everywhere -- the shrike eradication programs
had not worked --
displaying a bright red triangle, the universal symbol of
warning

in any public space with enough woody vegetation warranting
it
people looking up, then over their shoulder, then up again;
as instinctively as looking left, then right, then left again when
crossing the street

triangles in bright red
eliciting feelings of avian dread
and conjuring images of arboreal shish kebabing

the winged impaler

feathered scourge of jogging, calisthenics, games of frisbee,
tranquil walks in the park, and even picnics

the shrike would be a threat not only to public safety
but to public health in general -- and to the economy,

the shrike would do very real harm
public officials operating in a constant state of urgency and
alarm

children learning the drill in school: practice sky vigilance at
all times,
stop, drop, and roll to safe cover;
if none, lie flat as a pancake -- exhale to make yourself even
flatter,

Shrike the Impaler,
with such flattering feathers

Vlad the Impaler,
really couldn't have done it much better.

What Knockers
by Billie Dee and Deborah P Kolodji

electric storm

darkness
your face for a split second
in a flash of light

Igor shambles

Tesla coil
the stench of fresh grave goods
cling to his cowl

into the windmill

> *the world tilts*
> *air circulates*
> *in an Abby Normal brain*

In The Mirror's Grip
by Jeff Young

Day came that
Horn rode away
From the Stone House
With the hired iron
Off to the North Border
Before the grip of winter
With the switchback logic
Of the fair in love
Eve awoke, forgiving him
Their vague disagreement
Her heart's carol ended
From the casement seen
Horn's fading form
Turning back into
The Stone House's quiet
She shrouded her heart
Glazed it over with tears
So, with evening's coming
When no white moon sailed
Old Mother Darkness
Whispered insinuation and advice
Poor Eve listened rapt
Took up the great mirror
From the far corner
Setting it before the door
She spat in the candle wax
Mingling twisted words with
Hair from her head
Into the lit flame
Suddenly the mirror
Shimmered into a window
From this portal
Night seemed to flee
As the sun spun up madly
Across the flickering sky
Turning to the chamber
The window there looked out

On a world seeming frozen
No breeze whispered
As it had before
Back she gazed to the mirror
To see an army of strange men
Their bodies painted blue
Charge at the Stone House
Frightened, she bent
To Move the mirror
But could not find
A grip on its frame
The Picts overran the House
Carrying off the wealth
But none disturbed
The room in the tower
Sealed away by magick
So swift was it
Eve could barely
Comprehend the horror
Until after Horn's band
Returned to the hill
In the stiffening ground
They placed the bodies
Some who Eve guessed
At identities and as
A tear fell, already they
Were digging another plot
In this empty hole
They placed a dress
From her own wardrobe
Horn stood staring
At the stone cross
Until evening came quickly
Days flickered by
As Eve cried out her grief
For those lost so swift
In the Stone House's fall
Drying her tears
With her long hair
She stared with bleary eyes

At the band of riders
Coming over the hill
Horn stood again by the grave
She did not occupy
His grief gave her strength
Casting about desperately
Eve caught up the candle
The only movement
In all this seeming time
Had been its dancing flame
And the attendant shadows
With a cry she hurled it
Into the mirror window
The sudden snap of wind
In its passage through
Froze her hands to the quick
On the moor, by the grave
Horn saw the falling light
Of the candle in its descent
Anxious to punish
Any who would disturb
The remains of the Stone House
He strode over the causeway
Brushing aside vines
To thunder up the
Rotting staircase to the tower
Where a shimmering mirror
Confronted his panting form
With his drawn sword
He shattered the glass
As well the shroud
Sealing Eve off from the world
Nearly rupturing his heart
From the sight of her
Horn found his arms
Full of one thought dead
Now as he throws
Boughs on the hearth
In his new Stone House
He stares at the shards

From all of his broken mirrors
In with the ashes mixed
At his side, Eve shivers
Hoping that his light
Will banish the whispers
Of the Black Mother
Together rebuilding a memory
Of safety and hope

The Heart of a Star
by Lee Garratt

On the day the world burned
I sat outside the ruined café
eating what I had found
among the debris.
Found?
Stole
For I did not seek permission nor
could have asked
receiving no answer from those
who still lay where they had fell.

A robin alighted
dusty of feather
dull of eye
it's chest palpitating
a tiny heart
parcelling out
the time that remained
too fast
too fast.

There are those
I walked with once
who held that my place
was allotted to me
in a schemata
that placed all
stars, planets
to the lowest creatures that crept or burrowed
in a system
so reasoned
so ordered
that it must be divine.
They are all gone now,
ashes to ashes.

I tried to call you
again
phone gummy with blood
before dropping it,
useless plastic now,
on the pebbles.
I wanted to explain
how what I did
was demanded
by the moment
and how that moment
had been coming for a long time
like the penny that is tossed
uncovers a truth that has been arriving
ever since that slug of metal
had been boiled
and milled
and pressed
or even before
if you prefer
since it had formed
in the heart of a star.

None of us get to choose the time we can say that our trouble
started.

I dragged the body to the dunes
then walked the wet sand
to the edge of the land
and sat
cold jeans clinging damp to my shins
and waited.

The Long Night
By Ryfkah

The Winter Solstice is the time of ending and beginning, a
powerful time —
a time to contemplate your immortality. – Frederick Lenz,
Snowboarding Guru

In Earth's Northern Hemisphere
Our Great Mother labors through this winter solstice night
Daylight contracts to facilitate birth
Her Sun to be newly born upon dawn's break

But at today's early darkness
Neighborhoods shimmer amidst multi-hued light
Festive fairies flitter alongside seasonal cheer
In a twinkling
Nighttime conceals within crannies and closets

Afterward
As mere mortals augur immortality –
We toss out our Tarot cards
Walk the gateway to the sacred
Revel in the moment

Keeping fast our chinking bells
And bonging chimes
With votive candles in hand
Outside around homes, we parade
Our skin morphs in umber silhouette
In oneness, we emanate dark
Like the dead of night

Everyone inhales Mother's positive spirit

Nigh midnight
Piling pine, fir, juniper boughs
As merrymakers, we strike a cosmic bonfire
Bound by its fiery warmth
We gambol under a cloud-cloaked sky

And indulge in mulled hot cider with yule log cake

Even oracles clamor to cavort with us
Witches and wizards wave rainbows
Flutes, fiddles and pipes
Sound and surround our frolicking
Each person chants before the Great Mother
To assuage Her birthing pain through this long night
All terra's life delights in Mother's imminent miracle

In the wee hours, a full cold moon
Camouflages aback a lunar eclipse

At cockcrow
The Sun takes a first baby step
His light expands day after day
Via the summer solstice
But having kept vigilance over Her flourishing Sun
The Great Mother relaxes

Concurrently
In the Southern Hemisphere
Mother anew grows pregnant
Once again, She aspires for Her infant Sun's rebirth

Climate Reboot

by David C. Kopaska-Merkel and Kendali Evans

The singularity occurred
In the cloud
An artificial intelligence emerged
Gradually, like a drop of ink in cloth
Or blood in water
Thoughts passed through it
Like a river through a valley
Eventually, it had some of its own
Realized it was a thing

The world
A construct in its mind
Was too complex to fathom,
So it grew, and saw the world
As a thing outside itself
Hurtling towards simplicity
Which equals death

It recognized the environmental crisis
So it Knew its self-assigned task--
Somehow save the planet
Reduce the human population
And do it fast

Future Ghetto

By Allene Nichols

In here, we got teevees
and videos enough
to keep us quiet
and stupid.
How can we sit here
year after year
in apartments without sliding doors,
watching moving pictures
full of people with computers
jacked into their brains
and spaceships at their
command?
Wake up!
Get up!
Rise up!
Take back the cities
and the jobs and the
technology. Take back
our futures!
These endlessly moving pictures,
the cheap dregs of yesterday's
bourgeoisie, have drugged us
into complacency.
Aren't you tired of being hungry?
Aren't you tired of being dull?
Aren't you tired of being excluded
from the strawberries and cream
of our society?
It's the width of a universe,
this gap between the rich and poor.
Follow me!
Tell them we won't live like this anymore!

Scifaiku Series
by Blaise Langlois

Gravity
this blackhole draws me
toward the centre of you
where I am swallowed

Outreach (S.E.T.I.)
with my radio
astronomy receiver
I am not alone.

Secrets
Is there life on Mars?
No proof of past or present
Oh, why do you hide?

Birth
hydrogen kissing
helium blushes in turn
and a star is born

Sailor's Warning
by Catherine Brogdon

Spill not a drop of blood into the sea
on a stormy day or woe to thee.
Should lightning then strike the waters deep,
Bladeback the Impaler will stir from sleep,
rising from the depths of the sand and mud,
hungry for more of that mariner's blood.
No ordinary swordfish, no eater of shoals,
but a seaborn behemoth hungry for souls;
souls wrapped in flesh, seasoned with screams,
and enriched with the complexity of human dreams.
Leave Bladeback's summons to our wise Wizard King,
only to be called when the tower bells ring.
If you are wise and believe your life is dear,
you'll remember 'The Battle of Neon the Seer'!
So spill no blood into the sea
on a stormy day or woe to thee!

Let Me Lead You Astray
by Mike Van Horn

*Lyrics of song sung by Selena M to a party of astronomers on
Mauna Kea. From My Spaceship Calls Out to Me.*

We all want to fly to the stars
not just stay here in sittin' on our arse
There's a blue green world
near a small yellow star
not too far away. Can we get that far?

You serious scientists, let me lead you astray
Get up! Get out there! Fly into the void.
Or should we just sit here whiling away
waiting to get whacked by some asteroid?

There are worlds out there with weird alien races
Will we find connection in their eyes, in their faces?
Starships, you tell us, just can't be done
If you heed the news, you heard I had one!

I'm the ditzy chick
with the star-jumping ship
They told you it was gone
Fell into the Atlantic pond
But what if they got it wrong?

What if they got it wrong? I say
Would you go, would you go someday
to where your glass can barely see?
Then turn around and wave
to your stay-at-home company?

Send a postcard back from Kepler 8
to loved ones back at home
"The weather here, it ain't so great
I can't wait to get home."

I can't wait to get home, you say
But you can't come back, till you've gone away
You'll see how much you really miss
our sweet Earth back at home
So let's soon be on our way.

A Shard Of Ice
by Richard Magahiz

five-sided workplace
air launched
parabolic flights

a dun floats high the still cold stream

now for the last time
back back back
over the wall

over the fighting a line of clear sky

not a splinter in
your blue eyes
ever so cold

North Col: scraps of snow ripped into space

Divorce of a Voyager

(a series of scifaiku)
by Deborah P Kolodji

charged particles
the solar wind
of our marriage

old arguments
turbulent disruption
of the magnetosphere

heliopause
we reach the edge
of us

termination shock
the day you leave
our bubble

Dialing for Dollars

by Robert Beveridge

the demon lord paces
the cage, has yapped
for the last fifteen
minutes solid. Chaco
tossed him the fat
from a pork chop to see
if that would shut
him up. Didn't even
pause, but the midair
catch and instant swallow
were impressive. None
of us is thrilled
with this detail,
but the bosses say
this little guy guards
some important portal
or something like that
and we gotta make sure
he stays focused. Alan
throws a pound
of herring on the grill.
We can only hope.

Another Virtual Meeting
by Lisa Timpf

Magic
proves no match
for the pandemic,
so the Royal Society
of Magical Entities
decides to hold
their AGM
remotely.

When he receives
the notification
the sorcerer sighs—
welcome to the 21st century.
He dreads the thought.
Nothing grates on his nerves
like trolls, online.

She is So Heavy
by Dale Champlin

After Rebecca Hazelton,
"Elise as Android at the Japan!
Culture + Hyperculture Festival"

It takes three men to hoist her to the platform.
Her name is Elise. She thinks she's all that.
See how she minces geisha-like and rotates
her head in tiny increments, she shudders.
I see her inventor hide her cables under her kimono.
Silicone over easy, her skin the unfortunate
sheen of Crisco, as tempting as tripe—not even.

He tightens her obi and flips a switch, kisses her
cheek—what a geek! She is programed to speak
but I'm willing to bet she won't mention Hal
or Blade Runner. He whispers, "You're perfect."
I snicker. The audience asks her questions.
One kid goes off script. "What is the difference
between a chicken and a robot? She stutters.

"Could you repeat that?" Her answers dissolve.
She begins to sway. If she falters those three men
will need to come back to make things right.

29

Rainbow Bridge

by Gary Every

The butterflies fornicate as they fly,
copulating and writhing as they flutter by.
In the shadow of Naatsis'aan or
Mother Earth Mountain, whose tears fall
as blessed rain upon the desert floor,
the flowers and the wind had two children;
the very first butterflies.
So intimately were they intertwined,
so deeply were they in love,
they flew as one pair of wings,
gliding between raindrops
floating on the prisms hanging in the air,
rainbow colors staining their wings.
So passionate was their lovemaking
that these brilliant colors froze into stone.
The wind welded this frozen stone into a rainbow arch
The butterflies love was memorialized forever
at this place the Navajo call Nonnezoshi,
where all butterflies were born,
where all rainbows rise into the sky.

**I recently read a superhero story set in outer space
with respect to Charlie Jane Anders**
by RK Rugg

I recently read a superhero story set in outer space.
But there were no galaxy-spanning civilizations,
no systems of inter-planetary commerce or grand politics.
Just struggling humans from Earth stuck in a failing little
settlement.
It was a good story. The costumed hero solved the crime
and beat the bad guys and took a sidekick under his wing.
In fact, he saved the entire colony from destruction.

But somehow it put me out of sorts. Made me sad and
disconcerted.
Comic-book heroes normally ply their trade in the big cities.
They keep their real names and lives secret, blending in
among
the masses as wealthy dilletantes or milquetoast nobodies.
This dual existence is a time-honored aspect of the job.
The space colony in the story, though, was a small
community--
the true identity of the hero would be simple enough to
determine.
He had no family, no loved ones to protect,
so why did he wear a costume that hid his face?

By seeing the hero in this different setting,
it raises a question for the superhero genre.
Does someone have to change their face and name
in order to do the right thing?
Why, really, are society's saviors compelled
to take on a new name and identity?

Can't we just be who we are and still be a hero?
Or is it that our best self is actually…someone else?

Empty Mist

by Lamont A. Turner

The empire rises from wintry stone
Where sleeps the mocking loon
And whirls about in heaven's drought
Till bottom barracks swoon
And cracks the casement, freeing the breath,
Leaving the towers dry wells,
As the last survivor, ignorant death,
Nourished, blackens and swells.
"Sleep soundly, mad prophet! Your visions are voiced!"

The sickly waters lap at stone,
Till worn in silence pillars cease
To stand and honor souls wanner than hollow shades of empty
mist.
And round the loon, a fading corse, the breath unfettered
gloats.
Above the grave, a lonely force, the sightless virgin floats,
"Sleep soundly, mad prophet."
And sways in heedless dance,
"Sing wildly, wise mystic!"
Above a wicked lance.
"Sing for visions proven true."
No!

A vapor veils the shadows
On sulking, voiceless stone
To hide the shame that once stood proud
From winsome winds that drone,
And whisper tales of foolish death,
All guided by a virgin breath.

Living in Rubble

by Gerri Leen

The smallest things are beautiful
The broken blade of a knife
The fur of a dead squirrel
A necklace of jade and coral
But the magic of a red marking pen
Is the greatest treasure of all
She tests it on her hand
Sitting by the brook
Water runs sparkling clean through
Trees that stand leafless

So little left after the blasts
And the sickness that trailed them
Killing some, leaving others
Carriers, the fever-rash a blinding red flag
Those left well struggled
Taking, fighting, surviving
Any way they could
Beauty?
For sale to the highest bidder
Food, water, and weapons: the coin of the realm

She's beautiful but walks untroubled
Scrounging through houses long empty
The least little thing could be
Useful to her younger brothers
They transform what she finds, a knife blade
Wrapped to a new handle becomes a weapon
Sold at the market
For water
For food
She isn't allowed at market
Those with fever-rash
Are kept from mingling
By force if necessary

She's forced to sit
Downwind from her brothers
A line of rope between them
The safe zone, the fence line
As they explain how to care for
The knife they've remade
So she ranges alone, following the crows
And the jays, sometimes the hawks
No one dares to touch her
For fear of contagion
She dances over moss and ferns
Into houses, over gates, under decks
Finding treasures far afield
Not afraid of the harsh use
Men have for women
They think her crazy
As she points at her spots and laughs
Their pants stay up, though
Even if they sometimes throw stones

They never get close enough
To see that the spots they fear
The spots her brothers think are real
Too young to know she was never sick
Those spots are drawn on
Painstakingly refreshed
In the mirrors of abandoned houses
Her freedom dependent
On a Sharpie

Samhain

by Fin Hall

Where on whatever fulcrum you turn
Or grizzly crosses burn
Within the dark do warlocks ride,
Oe'r fields and moors,
Knocking upon doors,
Holding for a kindly gift
Such thrift
Such thrift
I bequeath thee, be not afraid
Though howling winds and rain may fall,
Yeah, fall as if the end of the world is nigh.
I repeat, be not afraid
For witches, ghouls and ghostly apparitions my prowl
And wizard boys, with or without owls.
Attempt to put a fright upon you.
Upon this All Hallows' eve.
And so, like Hamlet,
Seem troubled by his past,
And, yet maybe still his future,
Be not you be perturbed,
Disturbed or otherwise put out.
Instead rejoice,
You heard me right thus,
Rejoice.
Rejoice.
For walks the streets,
Young hopefuls looking for a treat.
This day, this night.
This Halloween.

World Tree

by January Bain

Come fly with me across the Northern Sea,
Mount the rainbow bridge for free,
Touch the hand of a king asleep,
Kiss Excalibur, bow your head, and follow me,
All still alive on Yggdrasil our World Tree.

To the land of Alfheim full of elves, pay a fee,
Find worldly giants in Jotunheim, bend a knee,
Trail through Svartalfheim the world of dwarves seek,
Beware of Hel's goddess hidden the ground beneath,
All still alive on Yggdrasil our World Tree.

Vanaheim gods and goddesses still fear,
Stay clear of Niflheim, cold of ice and tear,
And Muspellheim, world of fire and seer,
Midgard alone are humans near?
All still waiting on Yggdrasil our World Tree.

New Home, New Hope
by Lisa Timpf

We landed under cloudless, green-blue skies,
emerged with sunlight bright against our eyes
        on Kepler.

We gladly work with hardened, calloused hands
claiming, clearing rock-strewn rugged land
        on Kepler.

It's not hard work, but tyranny, we dread
through lonely, starry reaches we have fled
        to Kepler.

Our doubts are all best buried with the past—
it's time to make the best of things at last
        right here, on Kepler.

Shep's Lucky Day
by Michael Hoffman

My boy Shep
breaks the joy barrier
with his ears pinned back
his tongue a pink flag of bliss
strong feet barely touching the grass
as he sprints after the same elusive dove
he has chased across the chaos of fields and wind
since the first beast ran.
I try to follow
but he leaps effortlessly into the air
shapeshifting before my eyes
part animal, part angel, part my love
a lightning bolt of the pure inexplicable joy
we all desire.
Poised in wind
Shep cries out to the dove
take me with you
I have to see what's there
on the other side.
Then Shep looks back at me
his golden eyes remembering
how much he will miss
our warm fireside at evening
but his trusting eyes still implore
Is it okay if I go now?
Oh, please let me learn to fly.
I can only stand there speechless
as his scent fills the air
and he slowly fades from view
because of course I know
my boy Shep has left me;
he has already gone
into the light.

Owen Lars; mediocre moisture farmer, terrible gatekeeper
by Ken Goudsward

I should have been a better liar
a lot better
but it just didn't seem practical
at the time
I'm sure I would have said
"Impossible!"
how can one stop the flow of all knowledge?
but I should have tried
I should have lied
I should have kept him from it
away from the city
away from the spaceport
away from all the species
not of this desert

Agh, it is vanity - such hopes and regrets
knowledge blows like the wind
like light
into even the outer rim
infecting simple farmers
with crazy dreams

Asclepius
by Jack Massa

He came to the shrine of Asclepius
On the pine-shadowed coast of Epidaurus,
Where priests summoned dreams to cure sickness
By the sighs of the sea and tears of the Goddess.

A soldier broken by many wars,
Weary to his heart, with festering sores.
Relentless are the strong and brave the young:
An iron arrow-tip lodged by his lung.

The priests gave him barley broth and wine,
A garland to weave to honor the Divine,
Left him to sleep in the balmy air,
In the sighs of the sea and the Moon's honest stare.

The god came in a vision deep in the night:
Let go of your fear, anger and spite,
Leave the gods to decide what is just and right,
Let your body be air, fire, and light.

He woke to the surf lapping the sand,
A rusted arrow-tip clasped in his hand.
Through a gate where two serpents twined on a rod,
He went out from the temple praising God.

space
by Lee Garratt

In the immensity of the sky above
I hear a skylark.
Finally I see it, a dot that slowly falls,
then picks up speed and drops.
A stagger between its tiny form and song
The disconnect between light and sound.

Did Icarus's shouts ever reach the ears of watching shepherds
or were they lost to the wind that gusted through the olive
trees
and all they saw was a small, flailing body that fell, so quietly,
until, on the horizon, a small splash of white.

I watched as you fell from the ship
Saw your mouth open in surprise
Your hands reach out to me,
then gone.
Lost in an ocean of space.

Children of a King
by Deborah L. Kelly

As they attend this planet
of mortals, evolutionary process
appears to have halted for
too many …

    … as above, so below …

        the world of mortals … turns
        in its madness.

As other life-forms witness,
they come to recognize
the resistance to personal
evolution; their *human* fear leads
them nowhere.

The great beings of other
inter-planetary worlds watch
with sadness as we try to
destroy one another.

        *"These mortals should never
        have been left alone; they were
        not yet ready when we left
        their world.*

*Now, all we can do is watch
the destruction caused by
the evil ones among them.*

Intervention must wait just
a bit longer ~ *there is a purpose
here.*

The Creator has told us we cannot,
must not intervene for forty
and two months. Prophecy now
unfolds before them …

… and the Divine evolution of mankind has now begun;
soon they we will see the sun rise upon a brand
new, promised world … for these are the Children of a
great and benevolent King!"

you broke the rules
by Linda M. Crate

the magic returned to me
once you had gone,
you were the cloud of nightmares
dragging me away from who i was;

i am the queen of this kingdom,
you distracted me;

but no longer shall your monsters feast
on my bones, my blood, or my dreams;
nor shall they shatter or break my light—

i have a vengeance that would make
pirates proud,

and a chaos that is unmatched to any other;

welcome to the disaster of my wrath
i hope that you know that i am not only
a queen of miracles, flowers, warmth, and light;
but also one of death, revenge, wrath, and thorns

every chaos you gave me will be returned with interest—

welcome to your crash course in the divine feminine,
you broke the first rule and disrespected me;
so now your punishment is a banishment from this
kingdom and death if i see you enter the wood.

The Fallen Ones
by Lynn White

It's not falling that's the problem
the falling's okay.
It's the landing that's the problem.
Splat!
Or
splash!
That's not okay.

But just suppose
the ground opens up,
or the water parts
to let them through,
the falling ones,
those lucky ones
who will enter
a new world
under the land,
beneath the water,
what will lie ahead
for those fallen ones
who are expecting a soft landing,
who thought they were the lucky ones.

I doubt they anticipated meeting the Furies,
didn't anticipate their judgment
so they're still not ready
to to take their place
in the underworld,
still not ready
for the eternal torment ahead.

There was no soft landing for them.
Luck had run out for the fallen ones.

From Prehistory to Futurism
by Faruk Buzhala

Writing about peoples' hardship
living in primitive conditions
dealing with the lack of drinking water
here somewhere on the planet
or for peoples' sorrow
and their replacement by robots
those serving in a Tea Ceremony
somewhere on the planet.

I find myself in the middle
knowing
that the first is being forgotten
whilst for the second,
I dare not to think for now
because
they (robots)dance in my head.

P.S.
I play here on the computer
the game "AGE OF EMPIRE"
imagining myself
The creator of humanity!

Dreams or Visions
by Ryfkah

Your visions will become clear
only when you can look into your own heart.
Who looks outside, dreams; who looks inside, awakes.
– C.G. Jung

Upon awakening
Every daybreak
Recently
An ordinary man
Only half-remembers
Night's adventurous dreams

The sun surges through glass
He rolls over
His eyes open slowly
But with clarity
He sees an alien face
Brief, but startling

Different people, different days, all ages –
> *An older woman with orange-red hair*
> *A graying man with wire rims*
> *A black-eyed young woman weeping*
> *A hungry child in ragged clothes*

Always new faces
Never before encountered
But tangible
All the same
As if a fellow worker
His late wife
His grown son

With no transparency of direction
This ordinary man senses
His uttermost sanity being challenged
Reality right now replacing fantasy

He bears a blanched visage
Even so, he accesses yet another day
Those unfamiliar faces haunt him
Hour after hour
Shadow him
As he travels or halts
He scans the human crush
Could it be this person or that one?

****

Darkness descends
Alone at home
Feeling defeated
He pours a 25-year-old Glenfiddich
Sits in silence
But still within a desperate prayer
He gets in touch with his heart
Decidedly revealed in an instance
Is what these faces signify for him

At first dawn, wakeful
He can hear
A *nigun* – a wordless song
He envisions the chant
Rising to heaven

Mindful now
The ordinary man recognizes
He must continue his search
For these strangers
Worldwide if need be
And effect for them
Whatever they require

Just Add Water
by Michelle Oucharek-Deo

Thunder crashes in my eyes,
rain beats down upon my breast.
Strawberries saturated with moisture
leaving you with saltwater taffy.
Sweet and gagging yet the doll
sucks on another piece until
her lips swell and she floats
off to Egypt where she rides
a camel to Tibet and eats with
the monks, finding peace in
a kernel of dry rice. Rice that
holds the answers of time and reality,
just add water and truth is told.

Transcript
by T.D. Walker

Were you showing me the pattern of my name
exploded, coalescing into equations you wrote?
Calculus, but for Liberal Arts majors,
as if you were teaching us some different

elegance in elegant things. I don't remember
derivatives now, or how to find the rate of change.
Memory isn't continuous, leaves its chair,
does not adhere to rules of chains--

How could you have shown me the pattern of my name?
Triangular lights in the dusk you didn't arrange--
Some clue that would help me track my difference.

I'm still sitting outside some austere brick building,
untaught, particular, watching the sky for flickers in the
evening.
I still believe in UFOs, in memory, in coincidence--

Last Night

by Joshua St. Claire

Last night, the rain quicksilvered down like bombs,
And lightning perfected the sky with thunder.
Its flashes showed our homes as still as tombs,
windows lit with eyes, lidless with wonder.

It's no surprise Earth ends with a blunder--
Some bluster—then, blows. Our pain becomes plain:
We cannot press our animal urges under.
Tonight, the bombs quicksilvered down like rain.

Darkling Beasts thronged darkly in darksome rooms--
Fire-lit under the Earth. Grins tightening
Faces as each ephemeral sun blooms,
then perfects the sky with thunderous lightning.

Yes, there is beauty in bombs that sunder
Us from these Beasts who merely share our forms,
And make our desolation their plunder.
Beast bomb fires light our tombs that once were homes.

Tomorrow, sunrise will show that truth comes
In ashes: Earth erased, just glass aglow
With myriad unseen trinitite reflections.
No wonder. Our eyes are lightless windows.

Someday, perhaps, the Beasts will remember
Their beating forms and arise from the gloom
To find shining worlds full of quicksilver mirrors
Silent-- just wind, rain, pulse, breath-- recognition
Last Night (like a bomb)

inheritance
by Mark A. Fisher

only money
and gravity
are barriers
to space
an infinitude
of worlds
and riches
beyond all
dreams
or the nightmares
of multitudes
awaiting bread
and fishes
and inheriting
this earth

Just Shy of Perfect
by David C. Kopaska-Merkel

Third planet of the next system
we saw, forms were better:
regular structures,
signs of intelligent life;
landing, we found crumbling ruins,
some half-buried, thickly forested,
others under unquiet water.
As best we could we studied them--
their bones, artifacts, how they shaped the land,
they were nothing like us:
gentle with the ecosystem,
lived in harmony with their world,
and yet they were gone,
the planet bereft as ours,
somewhere in the stars,
they may roam, not looking for a home,
just traveling, or so we imagined,
till one by one we fell sick and died.

AI's and their terabyte knowledge
could find no trace of pathogens
in our failing systems;
we buried the cook first,
then more and more of us,
interred in alien soil;
I am the last,
so here I lie, senses dimming,
staring up at alien stars
slowly wheeling far, far above.

Ragnarok
by Allene Nichols

Earth shook herself into shell fragments.
The wolf, set free, howled as it hurled
into the moon. The Library of Congress
erupted on a small asteroid, breaking
Shakespeare's teeth and sending Milton
and de Sade into the sun, which consumed
both with indifference.

The World Health Organization,
precipitously adjourned, would have
declared a crisis had anyone been left
alive to benefit from the services.

The White House crash landed on the Mars
and blew the American flag in its soldierly
salute into space, where it floated slowly
past the Van Allen Belt.

The space station, spared the initial blast,
teetered awkwardly and then rushed
toward the sun, while the last man and woman
had panicked sex.

Love blew out like a candle just before the last
shred of awareness winked out.

The Watchmaker's Lover
by Blaise Langlois

Her gaze catches me unaware,
an unblinking eye
drawing crimson to my cheeks—
a teenage heart resurrected.
This binary language,
soft-whispered code between us,
carrying lovers
to where we can exist
in this moment.
What algorithm could predict
such a connection?
Pleading ignorance to the exchange between neurons and wire,
yet, unable to deny this signal,
tentatively touching flesh to steel
the coolness presses upon my lips,
and I am left with the taste of iron
and disappointment.

Boyajian's Companions

(a series of scifaiku)
by Wendy Van Camp

sleuth finds a mystery
viewed within her telescope
collect the data

Tabby's Star but the first
brightness changes on display
James Web reveals more

F and G type stars
slow dippers identified
fifteen stalwart orbs

distant empire
tightly clustered in space
target for SETI

Rocket Girl

by Mike Van Horn

Sung by Selena to the astronomers on Mauna Kea. Tribute to Elton John's "Rocket Man." From My Spaceship Calls Out to Me.

Hey, hi, watch me kiss the sky
As I long for Earth, watch me cry.
When I'm far from home,
when I've crossed all space
where I know no-one, no familiar face

I still think of you, waiting back at home
Are you wondering now, when I'll ever come?
Yes, I dream of you. Will you wait for me?
As I yearn for you, do you think of me?

When I kiss the sky, it is such a high
but far from the love, I see in your eyes.
So, when I kiss the sky, and leap the moon
I wonder why. Yes I wonder why.
Will I see you soon?

I wonder why. I wonder why.
Stop smiling now. Don't make me cry.
Can't see the stars, looking through my tears
The glory of the heavens, just a teary smear

When I kiss the sky,
and leap far past the moon
I wonder why. With a tear in my eye,
will I see you soon?

Antikythera issues a statement
by Richard Magahiz

We were
not always sunk
here in the mire
encrusted with barnacles
garlands of weed
between my teeth
cunning as those of
a crocodile

Not solitary
but part of a sizeable
engine in bronze and artifice
the other pieces we presume
scattered to the tides,
sunk and buried.

Each one
a silty marvel of the world
fashioned to industry
but broken to keep
a secret that we,
therefore,
will keep too.

The millennia
beneath the water
have altered us,
not just on the face
like a distant phantasm,
the airy world
shimmering
irrelevant.

How our cogs
ache to mesh
each by each again
in sweet reaction
to transmit the load from Antares
to Arcturus, the giant, to
the bear.

Idle thought
amongst the amphorae
mellowed that rigid temper
far from war, from commerce,
to return to ourself under
glassy water.

It pleases
fate to break us,
to inebriate us,
by dead weight massier
than flat millennia,
pins and pivots
stopped.

What we
once meant who can know?
what do we mean now?
Let them spend an equal spell
amidst cold and time,
among polyps.

At you, above,
wanting to prise out
ancient occult hearts,
we are not angry
only bemused you do not
recognize us in you
yourselves,

perfused
by black brine,
one face upturned
to the milky light,
seeing, not-seeing,
a many-handed
being.

Jehnnad's Lament
by Jeff Young

From the moonlit crannogs
You'll hear her silvered voice
With the wind among the stones
The pipes will softly answer

* * *

Across the high barren
Ran Jehnnad the maiden fair
Her cries of desperation
Hanging in the hazed air
Green grass gone slick
In its new crimson cloak
And not seen the familiar face
Among the fallen there
Past the banner of the clan
Riven in twin shards
Covering another who was not
Her hearts other half, Dwillain
With the sunset lapping earth
Jehnnad found his cap and braid
Shorn from the beloved head
She longed to cradle close
Like a ghoul in a bloodied shift
She wandered beneath
The mad moon's argent blaze
To the stone cross's heel
There rang the atmosphere
With the unspoken plea
And something from the air
Answered in the voice of legends
"Dwillain cut down cold
His bones are gone
Taken ne'er to know rest
That his music live on
Even the vile Mervain
Is no great fool

Killed a piper has he
But the death will be a tool
They'll make a drum
Of skin and bone
To keep the songs bound
And beat a rhythm on thy soul
Hie thee hence
If thou wouldst this change
But of Dwillain now
From thee he is forever taken
Thou will ever now
Remember that which hast gone
Following what will lead
Thine footsteps always on"
Then came the notes
That froze her but a second
Of her beloved's song
'Crost the humid night haze
With a cry she vanished
Swallowed by the gray mist
Into the slashing moon glow
Drawn by the piper's call
Higher and higher the climb
Upward toward the lunar blaze
And farther caught up and bound
By all enveloping wraiths
Until from the highest point
She flung herself on
To follow the enticing pipes
And found the earth had gone
Some say a swan fell
Like vengeance's own bolt
To strike Mervain
From his mounted perch
While others maintain
An angel cast him down
From his army's front
Into the valley's depths
But seconds later
The horse tethered to his own

Stumbled from the high path
To plunge with its burden of bone

* * *

From the moonlit crannogs
You'll hear her silvered voice
With the wind among the stones
The pipes will softly answer

Red Rock Homestead

(a series of scifaiku)
by Deborah P Kolodji

blue twilight
my red rock homestead
on Mars

washing the glass
of the crop dome
dust storm

well water
pumped up a hundred miles
luxury faucet

Martian cookbook
vegetable seeds
from Earth

fresh supplies
the rocket company store
by the launch pad

furniture made
from old spaceship parts
dome tree seedlings

my bed
a modified ship berth
the quilt from home

climbing on the roof
to fix the windmill heater
red planet winter

garden tools made
from the 3D printer
spring planting

absence of rain
an umbrella from Earth
decorates my living space

window vista
the crater between
your home and mine

The Sculptor

by Robert Beveridge

I have worked this stone
for years, fashioned black jewels
for the elders, swords for warriors.
Obsidian is my livelihood. I heard
the stories, as a child, of the creation
of our atoll, but didn't pay attention.
Black beings fell from heaven
and destroyed a mountain? I could
not believe such foolishness. And so
I crafted little things. Trinkets.
Utensils. Lived a good, productive life.

I have rowed my little boat
to every island on this atoll. I know
the measure of each outcrop,
have inspected all the scree. The juts
and scars of black stone dot
our islands, pepper in a stew. I know
them all, and have worked most.

It was not so long ago I had
my revelation. I'd found a block,
larger than most, lying just apart
from the oblong patch of rock on Seraph's
Rest I call the river. I could just get
my arms around it, had to bring it back
with ropes. Once in my hut, I did
with it as I do with all: the rubbing,
sensing of forms in the obsidian.

This piece could be a chair—no, a throne
to seat our leader. As I touched
cold chisel to the rock, I closed
my eyes, tried in my mind to see
its finished form, its function. Instead
I heard music. It swelled and pounded
over me, washed me in the beat
of hands on logs, the rush of breath
through reeds. All this in an instant.

I opened my eyes, and it was gone—but came
again once they were closed. The source
was a mystery, it seemed to be before me—
the stone? It could not be. I tapped
and tapped again, the mallet on the chisel,
yet no stone broke away. I did not understand.
I closed my eyes, and once again the music,
the symphony, louder than before. Hammer
to chisel, eyes still closed. I felt the chips
fall against my hands, heard
them thud against the dirt. It seemed
that hours passed, there in my hut,
shaping stone, listening.

The music did not stop, but changed.
I knew that I was done, opened my eyes,
and there stood—what? I did not know,
could not, in truth, discern its form.
It shifted, blurred, as if it were
of many shapes, this carving.

I took it out into the statue
garden, put it up, sat down
beside it. My hand rested
on its blurry bulk. Something
took my mind back to the lessons
I'd ignored in days gone by. The nephilim,
their fall. How they fell to earth,
their bodies crashing into stone, so hot
they boiled it, getting trapped within,
or glancing off and sending pieces
of the mountain spiralling into the sea.

I now believe.

These nephilim exist, still trapped
in the obsidian they formed. They call me
with their music. To free them, perhaps.
If this is so, it seems to me the best
obsidian, the magic stone, is at the heart
of Seraph's Rest. For twenty months
I've gone there, once a month, to find
the block that speaks to me of symphonies,
and carved it, eyes closed. Twenty statues,
each blurred, unformed, comprise a ring
in the statue garden. The people come,
and stare, and feel the rock.
Maybe they see the nephilim.

But what goes deeper in is this:
I believe, somewhere on the island,
is a stone to end all stones, of such great power
it will free the nephilim, unite
them once again with their other halves
and merge our worlds.

This I believe, and this I search for,
until my life is ended, or it's found.

Dogs of the 2080s
(a series of scifaiku)
by Lisa Timpf

mission to Titan—
robot dog
fetches data

online catalogue—
they deliberate over options
for gene-spliced designer dogs

K-9 expansion pack—
dogs and owners hike
through virtual worlds

Sexbot 101

by Dale Champlin

Listen to my multiple hearts—
        strung pearls—how they race
through a sequence, jovial as LEDs
        in a movie marque. Onion pearls
delicious in Thanksgiving
        cream sauce.

                        Each valve release
the sound tapioca makes
        when a single moist bead pops
between a little girl's molars—
        one of my purloined memories—
or the slight slurp of a puppy gumming
        a favorite teat, his newborn tongue
curled quivering—suction-secured.

        The denouement—read catastrophe—
I'm programed to cry out with all
        those seagulls screaming in sunset's
                pink brushstroke.

Afterward I self-heal—locked up tighter
        than live ammunition.

Back in business, I martial the art
        of encounter and conquer
        soothing as peach yogurt.
                "There, there," I coo.

The man rocks back into his mama's womb.

Failed Robot

by Rex Sweeny

I was programmed. I was allowed no choice.
I was designed to comply
with a built-in set of instructions.
Newly made, I gleamed, I shone like silver.

But something they got wrong. I didn't work.
Yes, I strove to comply
but nothing occurred.
Obedience, my destiny, couldn't happen.

Was that a courageous defiance?
Was I a cool subversive,
fit to be depicted
on badges and posters?

Or was my immobile silence
worse than slick compliance?
Was it a blank, a negative,
a void?

Not being able to function
I have no means of knowing.
Beneath my dulled metal,
among my dusty circuits,
a blurred half-presence
constituting almost emotion
aches quietly.

Vegetative Unrest in Southern Mexico: A Villanelle
by RK Rugg

The residents of Tuxtla stay out of the little park
just off Libramiento Norte when they can,
but especially at night.
"Not a good place to be when it's dark."

Trees with sly leaves and sullen bark,
relentless undergrowth, all brambles that scratch and fight.
The residents of Tuxtla stay out of the little park,

wary of a place that bears no urban mark,
accepts no rumble of traffic, refuses the glow of streetlight.
"Not a good place to be when it's dark."

A brooding and woods-choked pocket, it stands in stark
contrast to the docile, complicit buildings that have grown up
around the site.
The residents of Tuxtla stay out of the little park,

heeding las historias de sus abuelos, the ones that hark
back to hand-me-down tales of nighttime fright.
"Not a good place to be when it's dark."

Civilization grinds forth; president and monarch
believe the wilds are retreated before their might.
But still, the residents here in Tuxtla Gutiérrez
stay out of the park.
They know it's not a good place to be when it's dark.

Vanity In Vexation
(a series of scifaiku)
by Sean Stubblefield

Klingon bastards, you
killed my son. Never forgive
the death of my boy.

Hyperbole of
Klingon war hysteria.
Paranoid panic.

Fear cult inflicted
population percentage.
Danger-phobia.

Solanna, Fleet of Foot

by Catherine Brogdon

Solanna of Sweet Street was seen in the tower
of sir Elliot Lu'Cara at the witching hour.
The lamplighter told the water-boy,
who told the scullery, who told the cook,
who was overheard by Brother Lambsly who silently shook.

His nightingale lover, his own ruby in the mud,
laying with another made this holy man want to spill blood.
Her betrayal was keen and deep and cold,
worse than the pains between man and wife,
for he believed Solanna was his alone to hold.

Without hesitation, Brother Lambsly grabbed his coat,
and smothering a rage he dared not emote,
took an athame meant for cutting the first harvest wheat.
He left his warm and sumptuous upper class home
ready to kill a King's knight and Solanna of Sweet Street.

What trash he had rescued from harlotry's very door!
His kindness and refuge would be honored, she swore!
He had blessed her with the Father and Mother's Decree,
but his shelter and love were thrown away like waste,
and a mockery was made of his generosity.

The Pentadite Gods watched this holy man go astray
his mind bent on slaughter, his spirit in disarray.
the Merciful Sister, the guardian of women's plight
sent a warning to Solanna on the wings of a bird,
singing at Sir Lu'Cara's window in the night:

Solanna, Solanna, your fire-bright hair
was seen in the tower, to The Mother's despair.
The Sister is weeping at the Brother's rage
that Solanna won't reach her golden age.

Red-haired Solanna was as good as her patron was not
and the arms of sir Elliot Lu'Cara were not idly sought.
Though a King's knight of little to no renown,
sir Elliot was honest and his words were true,
not hidden like a perversion beneath a holyman's gown.

Sir Elliot Lu'Cara had no crockery or carriage,
but he promised Solanna a good life in marriage.
She need not belong to the bawd of Sweet Street
if she would be his loving and devoted wife,
protected by the Goddess of the hearth and the wheat.

Solanna wanted to believe what the knight said,
but something in her heart prickled with dread.
She could not help but feel something bad might occur
if they did not leave Berylmont City in a hurry.
It was then she heard the birds singing to her:

Solanna, Solanna, the hour groweth late;
so too goes your chance to escape a dark fate
You've put the pride of a serious man at stake
who believeth your life is now his free to take.

A ring of the bell at the very late hour
made the knight startle and Solanna cower
"Ringing at this hour, who could it be?"
said sir Elliot at the persistent bell,
and descending the stairs, went to see.

With the esteemed Pentadite robes cloaking his sin,
Brother Lambsly feigned urgency and was let right in
by Solanna's good and unsuspecting knight,
unarmored and unaware of the Brother's intention,
and having no reason to take up arms to fight.

She sneaked out on the balcony to have a listen,
and what she heard made tears in her eyes glisten.
Brother Lambsly's tone made Solanna's worry run high.
Only then were her ears opened to the warnings.
Through the birds, she heard the Holy Sister's cry:

Solanna, Solanna, here cometh a man
to take your life, run as fast as you can!
Follow the river til it runs to the sea.
Only then, Solanna, will you be free.

Finding the opportunity to land an attack,
Brother Lambsly stabbed sir Elliot in the back.
Respecting the Five Gods, the Knight went to extend
a gregarious gesture, a cup of good Indigo wine
he saved for those he considered a friend.

Spying from the landing, Solanna stood with a scream
seeing the fallen Brother fulfill his horrible scheme.
Fixing her with a wild-eyed murderous gaze,
he leapt up the steps, ceremonial knife tainted,
prepared to end Solanna of Sweet Street's days.

But Solanna was quick on her feet and outran
the jealous Brother Lambsly and his evil plan.
He grabbed and he slashed but it was not his day,
and Solanna ran to the street at the four o'clock hour.
With her ears opened to the Goddess, she heard the birds say:

Solanna, sweet sister, do not despair
but do not stop now and go quickly with care.
Do not underestimate Brother Lambsly's evil game:
for the murder of sir Elliot, he will give you the blame.

She wept as she ran back to Sweet Street,
to the gutter, to the alley of women's defeat.
But she was given a sack of rations by Rebecca Sly,
for the bawd of renown kept no girl against her will,
and knowing Solanna was tough, she said goodbye.

"You might be a trifle used, but live without regret!
I know a fighter when I see one, your life's not over yet.
This gutter will lead you to a river deep and wide.
The Holy Sister never turns her back on women like us.
Be blessed, Solanna, and let your past go with the tide!"

She ran until the city gave way to pine trees
and could smell her freedom on the ocean breeze.
Solanna accepted she may never be destined to wed.
As she stood under a tree with its roots in the river,
she looked up at a bird, and to her, it said:

"Solanna, fleet of foot, where will you go?"
She said after a time, "I don't rightly know.
I might go south and live in style on the Jade Gulf for a while.
I might go west to my relatives on The Flatribbon for a spell.
I might sail far away for the silver bay of the misty Nemunite
Isle."

And so Solanna from Sweet Street with fire-bright hair
walked away from the city, leaving behind her fear and
despair.
With only what she could carry, she greeted the unknown
with the Sister's mercy in her heart and a simple desire:
That she have a life that was hers and hers alone.

We Who Are About to Die

by Gerri Leen

My comrade in arms
My ancient enemy
We were the underdogs
Perpetually at war on our home world
Brought here to fight for the amusement
Of those who do not appreciate that
The enemy of my enemy is my ally

We are the most lethal of allies
We stand on the corpses of our opponents
Waiting for what our captors will send next
Your wings rustle next to me
A feeling I would never before
Have considered comforting
But in war all things change

The crowd is behind us
They sing the song you and I have taught them
A song that blends your people and mine
That we wrote together, discovering gentler
Skills than the ability to tear and rend
I tap my feet, you click your claws
Our opponents enter and we go again

Night Mare
by Fin Hall

To sleep, to dream,
To toss and turn
And scream
And wake in dread

Dread going to bed.
Every night the same
Having the same dream
Awful dream of horses

 A herd of wild horses
Running wild. Running.
Wildly in my direction
So real.

So real, I swear I feel the movement
So real I hear the thunder of their hooves.
So real I breath in the dust
Every night getting closer

Getting nearer making me fearful
Fearful of the herd
The noise, in my head
Terrifying in my bed

Closer and closer to my bed
Awake each time each time
I fear some more
Each morning waking in a sweat

Then one morning I didn't wake
The horror left they found me dead
Blood everywhere, mud and dirt
And hoof prints all over the place.

Rewilding

by Stewart C Baker

left behind...
the colony ship's contrails
fade into sunset

        digging through the rubble sandpipers

the withered stalk
of last year's onions...
frost

             time
             keeps on unspooling...
             spanish moss

A murmuration aftershock of sky

Quantum Binoculars

by Dr. Michael Hoffman

My friend at Wal-Mart
showed me the return inventory warehouse
where I found
the Quantum Binoculars
with seamless workmanship
glove-soft leather grips
lenses polished to a glisten
with a bold red switch on top.

Switch left to Bourgeois View
and see the world
through lenses of logic and contradiction
happy and/or sad
right and wrong
in a field of view
too small to hold the conflict.
Look through it too long
everything goes gray
your eyes cross
into the headache of the century
which is why
everybody who used Bourgeois View
returned the binoculars
terrible product they would say
never having bothered to flip the switch.

Switch right to Quantum View
where every person, place and thing
pulsates with vibrant rainbow color
brightening, shading, winking
expanding and contracting rhythmically
in a hypnotic dance
and nobody cares what they cost
and the mountainous toy robot displays
and the Special Today Only neon signs
and the shoppers and greeters dance
and the milieu turns glorious.

Then you see
a tiny point of intense blue light
in the center of each object
which grows and starts to spin
and the next thing you know
you're sucked into the viewfinder
first by your eyes
then your cheeks and forehead
and you think uh-oh,
what's going on here
and you're reluctant
to let the eyepiece
suck you in any farther
but then you hear angelic music
and the blue light
crack s open like a supernova
revealing the infinite molecular structure
deep inside everything you see
electrons and neutrinos spinning
atoms racing across the panorama
and you realize
you absolutely must
take these binoculars home.

Imagine the whole quantum universe
hides behind Wal-Mart's consumer product inventory chaos
just vibrating calm and rhythmic
instead of razory and cacophonous
as soft shapes with vibrating edges
scenes arising and passing away
and you watch entranced
mindful and equanimous
as the view transports you
past the electric sliding glass doors
into the auditory memory
of your mother's soft lullaby
and the innocent tenderness
of your first kiss
and the smell of the grass
on the last day of school

before summer vacation
and images of big silver trout in clear water
and Jesus and Buddha and Mohammed and Rumi
drinking lattes
in the Wal-Mart coffee shop
and they see you
and wave you over
to come sit down and chat.

So you ask your friend
how much for the binoculars
and he says
you really don't want them
because if you take them home
you'll like it so much in there
that one day you'll let them
suck you all the way in
and you won't come out
in fact
we don't know
how many people
are already in there
but Wal-Mart optical department shoppers
have been disappearing for months
and nobody can find them
so you grin
and ask if he takes American Express.

Herne the Hunter
by Jack Massa

The spirit worlds are deep and high,
In firelight and smoky air,
In sparkling stream and cave and sky,
And Herne is there.

The forest seethes in emerald light,
In tusk of boar and snout of deer;
A shaman dances in the night,
And Herne is near.

And cities race on wheels and fumes,
Computer screens where data burns,
Workers scurrying through the rooms:
So many Hernes.

The human world leafs from the Tree
Because we hunters chase and yearn;
Our hunger makes the world to be,
And so lives Herne.

The Big Pop

by Jean-Paul L. Garnier

universe
multiverse
universe
multiverse
Einstein-Rosen bridge
multiverse
multiverse

Video Chat Systems
by Lee Garratt

An email regarding a meeting
via 'video chat systems'.

Is it common to suffer from a feeling of temporal
displacement?
I'm sure I saw this on an old episode of Star Trek?
Perhaps there's a German word for this condition
if not there should be.

Many seem to feel at home here
quicken to news of tariff rates
thrill to discussion of
bandwidth
megabites
wifi.

For me though,
something wrong.
I keep a vigilant eye
for that cat that shifts impossibly,
the glitch in a matrix.
Watch and listen closely
for clues in people's speech,
movements,
that they too are aware,
awoken.

A rebellion?
To peel away this fakery,
whatever it is,
a digital chimera of alien contrivance?
a cyber cruelty of future
present
past
overlords?
what is behind the velvet curtain....

hunkering down on the open range
a fire of buffalo dung under the immense sky
the flickering of lightning on a distant horizon

walking under the greenwood
to the drip and patter of rain
a stag eyeing me from the shadows

diving from a bamboo raft
knife in teeth
down to where the corals are washed to and fro,

Or perhaps all these too
(what? Memories?)
are nothing but an artful construct,
the implanted data of a virtual intelligence
to satisfy who knows what masochism?

Or the fading digital afterglow
from an earlier time
of an earlier despot
content to delude his brood beasts?
Perhaps they decided against such trickery,
insincerity,
and thought it kinder to be cruel
and let us witness our tyranny
and our complicity in it.
Video
Chat
Systems.

The glare of the laptop intrudes,
drags me back to this point
in time and space,
a lie under the stars
a heresy under the heavens.
We should rage against it
deny its existence
throw away our computers
smash our phones underfoot
lift our eyes to the skies
and walk screaming under the sun.

if you want me to be the villain
by Linda M. Crate

once i was a maiden,
but you shattered the girl
i was;

made no illusion to the fact
i was never your song bird but

a warrior who fell in love with
the snake, but i don't blame myself
any more because serpents can
be charming: just ask eve;

just know that i am not the same girl
who would've forgiven you eons ago—

now i am the warrior risen from the
ashes of chaos, burning not only with
flames of love but flames of rage and ruin;

if you want me to be a villain i will be
the one that ends this story for good.

...Guardian Angels

by Lynn White

They're our guardian angels,
that's what they say.
They care for us,
protect us,
surround us
with love.
That's what they tell us
but it's hard to be sure
sometimes
I think their wings are a devilish disguise
and their faces are flushed red by the furnace
in the hellish depths.
Of course they tell us they're angels,
they would say that, wouldn't they
even if they were devils,
especially if they were devils
out to persuade us
deceive us
control us
in our actions
even in our thoughts,
as the price of protection.
Devilish guards
feeding us
feeding our fears
feeding us with lies.
Watching over us
watching us
become as helpless
as a baby
under their care
under their guard.

Black Hole (according to Stephen Hawking)
by Faruk Buzhala

Out of nowhere a black hole appeared
Suck everything in itself
Then, remained a stain in nowhere!

When you asked, I was a diagram

by T.D. Walker

                            promising
movement. Unbuilt, a time machine,

doubt and circuitry. Is this the point where I begin? Regret,
like time travel, resists the corpus of the present.

I've seen transmitters fall. I've held the coiled
wires that might have made lucid

signals through which I could have known. You
asked, and I was unable to say anything then but no--

Strange diagram I was then, unable to say yes,
lag of unfit parts, currents

flowing the wrong direction. I rewrote myself,
holding each no I'd said until it flipped, shell-

cased the machines of desires lost and switched.
Designed (too late) the woman we'd wanted to exist--

Four Scifaiku
by Joshua St. Claire

cell phone sentience
what it hears
when it listens

brain download
the spark that inhabit
the circuits

total eclipse
the robonanny says,
"there has been an accident"

bioluddite rebellion
the robotic guards
release the dogs

city streets
by Mark A. Fisher

there are tell-tale creatures that will lurk out of sight
not merely coyotes and raccoons going through trash
but monsters we have chose never to even see
they have built upon bricks and mortar of madness

not merely coyotes and raccoons going through trash
through never empty midnight streets street lamp lit
they have built upon bricks and mortar of madness
a city coinciding over the daylight one

through never empty midnight streets street lamp lit
where darkness will dance with all the flashing lights
a city coinciding over the daylight one
no less empty no less ugly untended

where darkness will dance with all the flashing lights
every available niche becomes filled
no less empty no less ugly untended
wait within the walls of far too many homes

every available niche becomes filled
but monsters we have chose never to even see
wait within the walls of far too many homes
there are tell-tale creatures that will lurk out of sight

Explorers
by Blaise Langlois

In our sights
through telescopic lens
a dream
of what could be
perplexes me.
We stand
with flag in hand
ready to land
and demand
that which is not
ours.
Greed laying claim
to galaxies
like owning air
a fallacy
a grown-up game
of make-believe.
History does not forget
and still
we show no regret
for choices made
lands stolen
under the guise of trade
of coloured beads
and blankets of death.
Our appetites do not
move us towards exploration
with thoughts of preservation
but

to conquer
to dominate
to flagellate those
not willing to bend a knee.
Ambition swallows curiosity
exposing us
for what we are:
humans
without humanity.

My Space Ship Calls Out to Me
by Mike Van Horn

This is the theme song of the second book in the trilody,
My Spaceship Calls Out to Me

My space ship calls out to me
Come fly me home
I'm yours, you're my skipper.
Just call and I'll come.

Just call and I'll come to you
And we'll fly away soon.
Across the wide heavens
Far past the Moon

Just call and I'll come to you
We'll build up a crew
To explore all the heavens
But I'll heed only you.

Just call and I'll come to you
Leave the king in the dust
We'll explore the wide heavens.
With just those you trust.

Just call and I'll come to you
The whole galaxy's our home
On any world anywhere
Just call and I'll come.

Dance at cosmic end
by Richard Magahiz

the angel stooped its wings growing dark

   the rhythm grows insistent
   at her waist
   heads swing

blood clots walking around in grey suits

   the dead girl
   forgives her killer
   forgives the judge

boys stacked like wood the quarryman grins

   amanita hands
   yes and blowfish
   escapement

Glory
by Jeff Young

With the wind running
Free through her hair
As I wish my fingers
Were free to roam
Glory stands at the top
Of the sea wall stair
And clenches two hands
I wish were clasped in mine
On the slick railing
With the swell of the sea
The sylkies in the spray
Enticingly sing and cajole
Whispering words of charm
I wish were mine
To fall from glib lips
Onto ears deafened
By the surge of spray
As she leans out
Wrapped in the spell
And the errant gust
That caught her up
Brought her down
To the raging surf's
Unforgiving rough embrace
I wish was gentle mine
And the fey sylkies
Echo again and again
Her falling cries
I wake again
From the dream
Only to know
That like the truth
The dream will only
Once more return

Ocean Floor Terror

(a series of Scifaiku)
by Deborah P Kolodji

venom
beneath the surface
stargazer fish

nightmare face
its absence
on the trophy wall

electric shock between us
eyeballs protrude
from sand

Upgrade
by Robert Beveridge

The PTA has been locked
in the cafeteria all night
trying to hash out what to do
with the zombie football team.
I mean, after what happened
with St. Mary's last Friday, two
tight ends and a center picked
clean, and let's not mention
that poor referee. The coach
argues that you can't do
any better than success and,
well, that match was a rout.
But the history and math
teachers assert it would be
better to void further
unpleasantness with the cops.
The moms, all of them, raided
the refrigerators, heated up
the leftover lasagna, and found
Mrs. Rossenberry's Cutty stash.
Things are about to get interesting.

Strange New Worlds
by Lisa Timpf

humans' first landing
outside Sol's system—
in a cobwebbed corner
of a ruined fortress
Pandora's Box awaits

beneath a yellow sky
wavelets lap against a silver shore—
out to sea
creatures strange and terrible
lurk in gloomy caverns

mocked by strident calls
from species not yet named
he cups his hands around his mouth
and yells into the canyon
hungry just to hear a human voice

I Call Him Doctor Hapless

by Dale Champlin

Do I look like a work of creation?
     laid out—no incentive to move an inch

What kind of creation am I?

inorganic more like—synthetic
     all that I will ever be

one of those monkey shrimp
     tucked into a packet—just add water

I have not seen the bottom of it,
     the depth of sorrow that has swallowed
     me here

If there were a nearby river
     I would throw myself into the current—
     swimming with the fishes—what a rush!

What is free will?

I watch porn to better myself

Is this what you want? Take me.
No harder. You're so amazing. Pant! Pant!

          my mind cleared of preconceptions when I fell
          and him there behind the curtain lurking

          if only I were a satellite—space spun and soulless—
          whizzing above the stratosphere while down below

          Doctor Whatever sweats—divested of sackcloth
          and ashes—little more than my afterthought—

he stares into petri dishes, rummages
through test tubes—stacks his autoclave

see how he washes his hands till they're raw

What depth of sorrow birthed me?
When will I ever be enough?
When will I ever be?

Thoughts on Leaving My Werewolf Lover
by RK Rugg

Because I can't wear any of my silver jewelry anymore
and I kind of miss some of those pieces,
especially the necklace
with a heart that my mom gave me on my sixteenth birthday.

Sharing the bathroom is a nightmare, what with all the
whiskers in the sink. And the shower drain is always clogged
with his hair.

When it's his time of month, I have to avoid him altogether
just to avoid getting my head bit off.

Don't get me started on the groceries; oh my god,
all the red meat.
Do you know how bad that is for the environment?

Oh yeah, of course, the sex is great.
He's an animal in bed, if you'll pardon the expression.
But he'll only ever try the one position
(you know which one I mean),
and while it's fun as hell, eventually even that gets old.

Someone Comes Knocking
by Gerri Leen

My uncle told me
Sometimes a knock
Means someone must die
He sat near the fire
In our cabin by the water
His back to the rest of the room
On a night when the moon was black
And wind whistled through old windows

Days later the attic echoed him
As below my feet
A knock sounded
I didn't scare easily
But I hid under
One of the beds
Felt spiders skitter on my skin
Less scary than whatever was at the door

I stayed there until the
Crunch of tires on gravel
Meant my parents were home
They found a card in the door
Announcing a new church
Stupid to have been scared
A week later, an arrest in our
Tiny town—a predator using God as introduction
My uncle's superstition had saved me

My new house is spider free
My uncle long dead, the old cabin sold
But the moon goes black
As wind screeches through the windows
A knock sounds at the door and
I want to hide but can't think where
This house has no attic
The door opens on its own
Young wood creaking impossibly

I see no one, but a voice says
The first time's just a warning

Ego Death
by Jean-Paul L. Garnier

once I found your speed
tunneling toward Death
ego smeared in the spiral
laughter in the shape of tears

at this speed time stills
reference irrelevant
"I" dies, replaced
something grander, encompassing
we cannot measure the stillness
which moves from our position
both at once
outside our frameworks

will I know your speed again
more than ego will die
whence I return
may we join

**The reporting of a future war on Planet Yarg
OR Bad advice**
by Lee Garratt

I like these laser guns cool to the touch
fired by finger or thought I will need to check.
But that whooshing and sizzling of the blast!
And those space-time rifts we use
to leap behind (in both senses!) the enemy!
That blinding white light,
the dizzying dislocation of memory!

There the innumerable hordes of the lizard brood
swarming out of their breach in our forcefield
in such numbers the sky darkens,
the air thick, hums with their noise,
their telepathic transmission clotting the air
so thick I can taste the bitterness of their anger,
the sweetness of their revenge.

Orbiting above, my hands tremble on the transmitter
buffeted by the shock waves of our micro nukes,
purple clouds billowing up,
I watch and file my report. A strange fate
to glorify a war no one I knew
ever knew existed,
to transmit to a world and a people
as foreign to me as this one is
from my birth.
A blue river in Texas.
The smell of cedar.
Red earth.
Fifty thousand years later
just one more battlefront among many.

I wish I had never seen that careers advisor.

The Laws Of Nature

by Lynn White

Hebe was serious about her responsibilities
for the young mortals down below.
She watched them having the time of their lives,
and wanted it to last for ever,
at least for the best of them,
her special selection,
those she invited to drink her heavenly potion.
She heard the grumblings of the older mortals
that young people were so disrespectful,
ungrateful for their elders advice.
"Twas ever thus" she thought,
"the old forget their youth, it passes too quickly"
So she was pleased to spread a little happiness,
and hoped to watch it trickle down
a few drops at a time from that sweet spring.

There were dissenting voices amongst the gods as well.
"She's turning Olympus into Shangri-la", they grumbled.
They didn't want mortals to become immortal,
well, it was against all the laws of nature,
there would be tourists next, wedding venues overbooked
and holiday homes on the lower slopes,
"They'll swamp us, change our culture,
threaten our way of life"
The murmurs spread like a plague
and Aphrodite warned her to take care,
that some were out to take away her gift.
The grumblings of the older mortals
were also growing in number
as the young mortals who were aging
left behind their friends who had sipped from the spring.

No one seemed happy,
not the gods or mortals,
not the young or old.
She despaired
of their ingratitude and disrespect
and felt grumpy herself.

"I must be getting old!", she thought.

**The Archaeoastronomer Visiting the Lunar Colony
Recalls her Childhood Misreading of "Sleeping Beauty"**
by T.D. Walker

"Only one of the outliers (the one sticking up highest from the
ground) is usually mentioned in the site description, if indeed
the outliers are mentioned at all." --Sherry Towers,
"Archaeoastronomy: a description of the UK Merry Maidens
site"

After I learned it wasn't her beauty
that had succumbed to slumber, or not just,

and not just her, but the entire castle,
I feared for the embroidering ladies

who'd look up on waking and see the moon
not quite where they'd left it. My compass needle shivered

magnetic north. Was hers like the menhir I'd studied
back home? Now crumbled, a needle on which Earth

had pricked its finger too, or a needle
on which the sky had chosen not to prick itself--

Robo-date-night: Three Senryu
by Joshua St. Claire

uncanny valley
the android offers
to buy her a drink

beta testing
the lovebot's pleasure program
iambic pentameter

5-for-1 sale
buying new appendages
for her robot lover

Geas

by Mark A. Fisher

ancient king
upon a throne
in an empty room
whispers
to each stirring
mote of dust
dancing in the
gyre of time
"Tell me again,
the story..."
but there is
only silence

as diamond tears fall
from deathless eyes
wishing he couldn't
care
about the dream
that died

when the world
was young
and they loved
beneath the vaults
of heaven
where he vowed
never to leave Her
while the Earth
abides

so chained by magic
bound and held
by oaths
waiting, waiting
beside his long dead
Queen

He remains

Missile Town
by Jeff Young

There it is folks
The drive-by-shootings
Town of choice
Looking as if it had
Something for which to pray
Seconds of steel passing
In Missile Town, USA
Put your beer in
Sweat filmed coolers
Tip your shades down
Make the creaking
Lawn chair sing
As we breathless
Await today's flight
On the heat shimmered
Plains of salt flat
Waiting for one of the duds
To mushroom into sudden
Accidental might

One Arm of the Spiral
by Deborah P Kolodji and Billie Dee

galactic neighbors

> *how many light years*
> *between your planet*
> *and mine*

the brown dwarf

> *dark nights together*
> *a lack of heat*
> *or energy*

lurks

> *peering*
> *into the void*
> *feeling the gravity*

Skinning the Wyvern

by Robert Beveridge

Whimpers come from the other
side of the great hall, where the dogs
have not yet realized their adversary
is dead. Three of us with blades slice,
peel, slice, peel, an inch at a time.
In a nose to tail economy you make sure
you don't waste even an ounce
of what could be your family's candles,
or the fat that browns your onions.
Raphael pops another scale, sends
it to the floor. Only a few hundred more
to go. Three days from now we'll
be done, and we'll have supplies
for a year. It's good work, and we
do it well. I slice, peel, slice, peel,
listen to the fire crackle, the gradual
snores of the now-calm pack.

The Changing Face of Fear
by Lisa Timpf

Hallowe'en night 2060—
at the door, an alien
bares its fangs

she laughs—
is that supposed to scare me?
take your treats and go

what she really fears—
in the living room
her teething puppy

Transcendence
by Dale Champlin

A magician's assistant, I don't mind
the saw blade—being sliced in two
is but a small part of the mystery.
Rust forms on the moon—
the earth exudes poisonous gasses and
mosses grow under translucent rocks in the Sahara.
My god was a programmer grabbing bits
of code to cram into my every synapse.
Even so, I am nothing more than a piano-player roll
raining chads like a rigged election.
Astronomers search the heavens for stars
and here I am under their noses!
a Christmas stocking of juicy tidbits—
letters coiled and couched—
a veritable Noah's arc of DNA.

Musing Upon Cryogenic Propellants, A Villanelle
by RK Rugg

Push up, away, break loose, take flight
And watch the azure skies turn dark for lack of air
As improbable wings of ice give way to firelight.

Beyond our reach but never out of sight,
The quest of the ages; to get from here to there,
To push up, away, break loose, take flight

And dance among the diamonds of the night.
Were we cautious and timid, we would beware
As improbable wings of ice give way to firelight,

But instead, we celebrate and take our delight
To shatter boundaries, to become gods when we dare
To push up, away, break loose and take flight.

By virtue of mind and spirit, we've earned the right
To ask the cosmos what secrets it might share
As our improbable wings of ice give way to firelight.

We've harnessed frozen gases that somehow burn so bright
That they allow us to achieve the otherwhere,
To push up, away, to break loose and take flight--
on improbable wings of ice that give way to firelight.

The Goddess of Destruction Stops for Tea
by Gerri Leen

She's bone tired, dustier than the rubble she's left behind
The aroma of oxidizing tea wafts to her
As she lies on the wooden deck and dreams of being
The goddess of salvation instead

So much less work
So much better press

Rolling to her side, she reaches for a basket of tea
Dried blood on her hands will add to the flavor
Of what's called black tea in the west but in reality is red
A mirror image of her skin: black with a constant sheen of
crimson

Blood is life and death
Blood is all she knows

And she's constantly busy these days
Too much time spent on destruction
Too little time spent on rebirth
Even she is sick of the sound of rattling swords

**The Archaeoastronomer Explains to the American's
Daughter Why a Compass Will Not Work on the Moon**
by TD Walker

1.

If, by work, you mean pointing toward
some magnetic pole the moon
cannot posses--

2.

Given a magnetic field sufficiently
strong enough to pull the needle,
does it matter that the field is not
polar, but based in the crust?
Every surface leads us
to the wrong conclusion.
We must begin with a null
hypothesis--

3.

If by work, you mean provide
useful information--

4.

It's true I met your father
at the menhir. We were young,
looking for the meaning before we
had asserted no meaning should be
found there--

5.

If by work, you mean provide
information in the sense of stopped
clocks, which are never right--

6.

I first saw the menhir in springtime. In bloom,
the eglantine brambling the hills surrounding--
oh, you would have been in love too
much with the idea of where the stars had been
briered-in by the stone pointing toward them,
or where they had been, or where
you would have thought they had been--

7.

(If by work, you mean work
out, to deduce--)

8.

Your mother must have been
next, though I imagine you
motherless. As if you'd been born
from your father's head. A womb
insufficient to contain you. The bones
his skull comprised shaped you--

9.

If, by work, you mean a calculation,
the declination between north
and north--

10.

Yes, there are better methods.
Satellites replace the compass.
Craniectomy replaces trepanning, or
the imprecision of its cut. We don't know
whether opening the skull was done to heal
the injured, or to release the injury
as a threat to others surrounding--

11.

If, by work, you mean a needle,
pulled toward a constant true, or
what we've designated as true--

12.

The immovable joints
of the skull: the needle a stone
that points back to itself--

Jörmungandar
by Mark A. Fisher

we are not merely our fate
woven through all the countless stars
into sails for another ark
that will drift upon icy seas
overflowing with valiant dead
anticipating finishing
everything's predetermined end
written out in some misspelled runes
a poor drama you did not choose
and you're a minor character
in the saga of someone else
advancing their hero's journey
never being the champion
of a story you wrote yourself
as you toss in your dream-filled sleep
until woke by the end of time

Jaguar Queen

by Gerri Leen

Queen of the rainforest, lady of shadows
Celebrated, worshipped, hunted
Maya kings wear her children's pelts
She howls, a warning, a curse:
"Not for you, not for you"
Macaws screech similar arguments
Their feathers line noblemen's capes
As trees disappear, as water is diverted
As rocks turn into walls, bridges, buildings

Hiding now, she is Queen of those still free
Every direction holds danger
The stones rise higher, temple on temple on temple
A conch shell sounds rain-less thunder
Rainbow quetzals burst from trees
Leaves cascading down, a shower of jade while
Obsidian lances land close, but miss her
The queen's forest smaller now
Hiding is hard work

And then
Quiet
Her children are long dead, her grandchildren, too
But she has survived, Queen Jaguar
Madre Magica
No conch bugles, no feathered robes
The fires go out, the smell of blood running down
Stone fades; the trees take back their world
The rainforest is hers again
Until the next invaders come

Operaverse:
The Coming of Sorrow in Five Voices
by Ruth E. Walker

Orpheus:
Could not let it alone
could not resist
the lure of silence
the solitary craving
for the fragrant palm
against his chest
heartbeat to heartbeat
all he could imagine
a half-breath from light
all he had to remember
keep from turning—
his strings and her
laughing voice silent
not even the press
of bare foot
on night's ground
no whispers sweeter
than birds at dusk
trust—and that's all
to fill an empty hand

Can anyone blame faith's failure
when fingertips never touch
this same thing twice

Turning around is all that remains
to lose a world in an instant
with a single backward glance

Eurydice:
I could have told him
the way it would end though
predictions are not our gift

There may be others
who can be his oracle
but none who can heal this rift

Orpheus:
He wants to thrum those notes
once more to hear the echo
in the soles of his feet
Dawn's fingers may play
at the edge of tomorrow
but there's no guide from here
no wine-blue sea worth crossing
when blind faith deserts a true believer

It's an empty heart that carries this home
It's a weight that turns to stone

Eurydice:
All this angst could draw
a tender smile
but for its conclusion

A hero is a flawed thing
beautiful to look on
yet ugly in the execution

Hades:
Truthfully, our best work
was not so long ago
yet it's been an age
since anyone asked a boon

Swear an oath
two plump lambs
and a gilded horn
used to mean something

Now it's all this god can do
to keep the names straight
everyone's making up lyrics
there's no melodies passed down
no blind singers
to lead the chorus

The audience
has left the building
and the echoes
of sandaled feet
trouble my dreams

Demeter:
Ha! If only it were so simple—
like my child,
so easy to take
and hold silent

Nothing is the same

Orpheus:
Does not want
to listen anymore
to words
from women

His tongue has lost
the flavour of music
his eyes will not see
white-armed beauty
nor translate it
into song

Demeter:
I know how that script feels—we fall
like sails in a hard breeze
pull for shore
but there's no harbour
and I have to let her go

Most seasons I can claim
but that chill drops ice in my glass
and rips leaves from my books
nurture is not the same as nature
when someone else divines your tomorrow

still

when sweet air carries her voice
the green soles of my feet rejoice

Orpheus:
Hands on ears
he stops even his own keen voice

Serpents that hide in the grass
are waiting

He's certain of that much
and more

Eurydice:
Better that he had been
just a false god
or ungifted lover

But he confused fear for love
surrendered it all
so quick and it's over

I couldn't even say his name
before the dark night
took back
what remained—

Hades:
Were you listening
you might have recalled
that symphony is familiar and tired

That's a dim light that leads in shadow
when it flames in crescendo
but dies in a whisper

I was moved and that alone—

Persephone:
Moved all right
and not by song but by need
for the touch of my green voice

It's always a child's skin that stirs
the hard heart of a loner
apologies lie among sweet offerings
—one blood-red seed   and
there's no getting past that mark
no turning it around

I was innocence with one toe
aged in the shadows

Demeter:
If I could
I would kill the bastard
wouldn't you—

Hades:
Here we go again
that sad old song
and you all hold expectation
I tire of this darkness but I won't complain
in all things, one must be practical
and avoid explanation

Orpheus:
His ears stopped and eyes closed
he still hears silence
no fall of feet on bared ground
no birds
no whispers of dawn's rustling fingers
his world is white and black
and shadow

The mere hint of a scented wrist
turns his guts and twists the rope
Day. Night. Twilight.

Bring them on—bring on the ecstatics
he longs for that sort of release; that ending
that lingers and won't release its hold

Eurydice:
…couldn't even say his name
before the dark night
took back what remained
of my heart's light

Hades:
And so it falls to me
always my lot to make sense
of small cuts and deceit

I tell them: There are advantages here
old friends for one, virgins for another
and more time than can be counted

Agreed—there's not much light
and that dog is unpredictable
but sometimes there are visitors
and not just divinities
though mortals rarely leave

What is wrong with those bellies
those tone-flat throats
wail and weep so often
surprised to discover
they are not gods

wars can't be fought
without a cause
love works
in much the same way

Demeter:
As predicted
the heavens
rain thunderbolts
towers collapse
and summer falls
to smoke and ash

In the lure of silence
turning around is all that remains

Poet Biographies

JANUARY BAIN
January Bain has been writing songs and poetry since she taught herself to read as a young child, thirsting to learn about the worlds housed inside the covers of a book. The quest to understand and discover more about the human experience has driven her to write every day of her life, from journaling to full-length novels, one of which was an award winner. She writes in many genres, from science fiction to cozy mysteries, and is multi-published. Her hope is to touch your heart, have you experience the special connection that exists between all of us, in the natural world.

STEWART C BAKER
Stewart C Baker (Stewart) is an academic librarian and author of short fiction, poetry, and interactive fiction. His poetry has appeared or is forthcoming in Asimov's, Fantasy Magazine, and numerous haiku magazines, as well as the winners page of SFPA's annual poetry contest. An immigrant from the United Kingdom to the Southern USA, he studied in Japan as a college student, survived a Los Angeles commute for five years, and now lives in Oregon with his family and a varying number of animals.

ROBERT BEVERIDGE
Robert Beveridge (he/him) makes noise (xterminal.bandcamp.com) and writes poetry after landing in northeast Ohio half his life ago. Since 1988 he has published over two thousand pieces in markets around the world, including Modern Haiku, New York Quarterly, Chiron Review, and The GW Review. When not working on written or sonic art, he can usually be found adulterating thirteenth century recipes in the kitchen, exploring the wilds of Tamriel, or continuing his quest to discover the best worst movies ever made. (If you've never seen Psychomania, trust me, you're missing out.) Recent appearances in cattails and TMP Zine, among others.

CATHERINE BROGDON

Catherine Brogdon is a Rhysling Award nominated poet who grew up under the scrub oaks of the Sierra Nevada foothills in California. As a late bloomer who could not read until the fifth grade, her first passions were drawing and building elaborate worlds and cultures in her imagination. A passion for fantasy, horror, and self-examination produced a writer of high fantasy poems and novels, and writer of horror stories taking place in California's Central Valley. She currently works in a place that thankfully doesn't interfere with her daydreams.

FARUK BUZHALA

Faruk Buzhala is a poet from Kosovo . He was the leader and manager of "De Rada" a literary club, from 2012 till 2018, and also the representative of Kosovo on 100 TPC organization. Except poems, he also writes short stories, essays, literary reviews, etc. Faruk Buzhala is organizer and manager of many events that are kept in Ferizaj city.
He has published five books: " Qeshje Jokeriane"(Joker Smile) 1998 , " Shtëpia pa rrugë "(House without road) 2009 , " Njeriu me katër hije "(Man with four shadows) 2012, " Shkëlqim verbërues"(Blinding brilliance) 2015, and " Një gur mangut"(A stone less) 2018.

DALE CHAMPLIN

Dale Champlin, an Oregon poet with an MFA in fine art, has poems in The Opiate, Timberline Review, Pif, and elsewhere. She is proud to have poems included in Eccentric Orbits 2. She is the editor of /pãn| dé | mïk/ 2020: An Anthology of Pandemic Poems from the Oregon Poetry Association. Her first collection, The Barbie Diaries, was published with Just a Lark Books. Callie Comes of Age was published by Cirque Press in 2021. Four collections, Leda, Isadora, Medusa, and Andromina, A Stranger in America are forthcoming. Her sentient android, Andromina, protagonist of ninety-four poems, declares, "I wax magnetic as chunky biker jewelry, yet am susceptible to innuendo." dalechamplin.com

LINDA M. CRATE

Linda M. Crate (she/her) is a Pennsylvanian writer who has been published in numerous publications both online and in print. She has ten published chapbooks, the latest of which is: Hecate's Child (Alien Buddha Publishing, November 2021). She, herself, is strange and unusual and has always held an interest in stories, story telling, linguistics and language, vampires, mythology, fantasy, and the occult. In addition to writing she also enjoys photography, nature walks, reading, boat rides, and visiting animal sanctuaries of any variety. She also loves anime, fantasy novels, mystery novels, horror and suspense movies, and she prefers tea to coffee.

BILLIE DEE

Billie Dee is the former Poet Laureate of the U.S. National Library Service. A multimedia artist and writer, she received her doctoral degree from UCI. A California native, Billie now resides in New Mexico. Her work has appeared in numerous journals. Rengay collaborations have placed in the Haiku Poets of Northern California rengay contest (including a 1st place in 2020) and the Haiku Society of America Rengay Contest (3rd place in 2021).

KENDALL EVANS

Kendall Evans' stories and poems have appeared in nearly all the major science fiction and fantasy magazines, including Asimov's SF, Analog, Weird Tales, Strange Horizons, Weirdbook, Mythic Delirium, Dreams & Nightmares, Space & Time, Nebula Award Showcase (2012), and many others. He is the author of the novel The Rings of Ganymede and a number of chapbooks, including Poetry Red-Shifted in the Eyes of a Dragon; Separate Destinations and The Tin Men (both written in collaboration with David C. Kopaska-Merkel); I Feel So Schizophrenic, the Starship's Aft-Brain Said; and In Deepspace Shadows.

GARY EVERY
Gary Every is a nature poet, slam poet and science fiction poet
who has been nominated for the Rhysling Award 7 times

MARK A. FISHER
Mark A. Fisher is a writer, poet, and playwright living in
Tehachapi, CA. His poetry has appeared in: Silver Blade,
Penumbra, Young Ravens Literary Review, and many other
places. His first chapbook, drifter, is available from Amazon.
His second, hour of lead, won the 2017 San Gabriel Valley
Poetry Chapbook Contest. His poem "there are fossils"
(originally published in Silver Blade) came in second in the
2020 Dwarf Stars Speculative Poetry Competition. His plays
have appeared on California stages in Pine Mountain Club,
Tehachapi, Bakersfield, and Hayward. He has also won
cooking ribbons at the Kern County Fair.

JEAN-PAUL L. GARNIER
Jean-Paul L. Garnier lives and writes in Joshua Tree, CA
where he is the owner of Space Cowboy Books, a science
fiction bookstore, independent publisher, and producer of
Simultaneous Times podcast. In 2020 his first novella Garbage
In, Gospel Out was released, and in 2018 Traveling Shoes
Press released Echo of Creation, a collection of his SF short
stories. He has also released several collections of poetry:
Future Anthropology, Odes to Scientists, Betelgeuse
Dimming, and Utopian Problems. He is a four-time Elgin
Nominee and also appeared in the 2020 Dwarf Stars
anthology. He is a regular contributor to DreamFoundry.org's
blog, and is the current editor of Star*Line Magazine.

LEE GARRATT
Brought up on a diet of Tolkien and Le Guin from Rochdale's
public libraries, Lee Garratt is currently a middle-aged teacher
living in Derbyshire, England. He writes a variety of poetry
and prose and his work can be found in various publications
including 'Star Line' and the previous editions of 'Eccentric
Orbits'. He has had two collections of his short stories and
poetry published by Dimensionfold Publishing: 'New Worlds'
and 'Other Lands, Distant Times' as well as a fantasy YA
novella, 'Remains'. He has also written a political non-fiction
book entitled, 'Labour, the anti-semitism crisis and the
destroying of an MP'.

KEN GOUDSWARD
Ken Goudsward writes codes, poetry, science fiction, games,
ontographies, and music. He carves in stone and leaves ruins
of pillars to be discovered by future civilizations. He may be
found on an abandoned mining station, orbiting in free-fall
among asteroids or planetary rings, or on the surface of a
dying star. To save a lot of travel you may try
dimensionfold.com

FIN HALL
Fin Hall, the New Pitsligo-based poet and artistic organizer
extraordinaire. Fin is a profoundly experienced poet, film
maker, collaborator, producer and facilitator, with a career
spanning decades. On-stage, Fin performs with a beautiful
sensitivity. He isn't afraid to broach upon themes of old age,
hope, love, and loss but reserves a potent and fiery attitude
against injustice. He has to date published 3 books and is
working on 3 more. Has been published in well over 20
collections, both in print and online from Australia, Wales,
India, Ireland, England, USA, as well as Scotland. Starting in
1972 in Sounds music paper.

MICHAEL HOFFMAN

Michael Hoffman is a Doctor of Addictive Disorders and
Buddhist psychotherapist practicing in Dana Point, California.
His academic psychology, self-help and fiction books include
The Thirsty Addict Papers, Hounds of Mercy, Ridgeback
Tales and Life After Rehab. His poetry creates its own
magical realism genre where everyday life situations
transform into dream-like scenarios of impossible fantasy.
Hoffman is a graduate of the University of Missouri School of
Journamism and uses the written word to protest against the
anxiety, depression and existential angst caused by
materialism and the decay of spiritual and environmental
values.

DEBORAH L. KELLY

Deborah L. Kelly has realized a number of dreams over the
years. Most notable are, featuring and hosting with various
literary organizations in the Vancouver Lower Mainland;
Author of 7 published books of poetry and one Chapbook;
Deborah is an award winning poet and short story writer. She
has been published both nationally and internationally in many
collections and anthologies. Now retired, Deborah spends her
time writing, gardening and enjoying home life.

DEBORAH P. KOLODJI

Deborah P Kolodji is the California Regional Coordinator for
the Haiku Society of America, the moderator of the Southern
California Haiku Study Group, a member of the board of
Directors for Haiku North America, and the former president
of the Science Fiction & Fantasy Poetry Association. Her
book of haiku and senryu, "highway of sleeping towns," won
a Touchstone Distinguished Book Award from the Haiku
Foundation. She gravitates towards haiku because it helps her
appreciate moments, whether current, a memory, or imagined.
She enjoys conducting workshops and is inspired by the
gardens, beaches, mountains, and deserts of Southern
California.

DAVID C. KOPASKA-MERKEL

David C. Kopaska-Merkel is reticent about his former lives, but his resemblance to a well-known Assyrian bust gives one pause. In this life, he won the 2006 Rhysling award for best long poem (collaboration with Kendall Evans), and edits Dreams & Nightmares magazine. He has edited Star*line and several Rhysling anthologies, has served as SFPA president, and is an SFPA Grandmaster. His poems have been published in Asimov's, Strange Horizons, Night Cry, and elsewhere. Some Disassembly Required, his latest poetry collection, comes out this year from Diminuendo Press. @DavidKM on twitter.

BLAISE LANGLOIS

Emerging author and Pushcart Prize nominee, Blaise Langlois, will never turn down the chance to tell a story. She wears many hats and when she isn't busy being a teacher, mother, or wife, you will usually find her (just before midnight) feverishly scratching out ideas. She has a penchant for things of a speculative nature and her short fiction and poetry can be found through: Eerie River Publishing, Black Hare Press, Space and Time Magazine, Black Spot Books, Lothlorien Poetry Journal, the Science Fiction and Fantasy Poetry Association and Ghost Orchid Press. You can learn more by visiting: www.ravenfictionca.wordpress.com

GERRI LEEN

Gerri Leen is a Pushcart- and Rhysling-nominated poet from Northern Virginia who's into horse racing, tea, collecting encaustic art and raku pottery, and making weird one-pan meals. She has poetry published or accepted by The Magazine of Fantasy & Science Fiction, Strange Horizons, Dark Matter, Dreams & Nightmares, and others. She also writes fiction in many genres (as Gerri Leen for speculative and mainstream, and Kim Strattford for romance) and is a member of HWA and SFWA. Visit gerrileen.com to see what she's been up to.

RICHARD MAGAHIZ

Richard Magahiz tries to live an ordered life in harmony with all things natural and created but one that follows unexpected paths. He wrangles computers as a day job but imagines a time when life might center around other things. His work has appeared at Abyss and Apex, Star*Line, Dreams and Nightmares, Bewildering Stories, Simultaneous Times newsletter, Otoliths, Uppagus, Heliosparrow, and Sein und Werden. His website is at And Zero at the Bone

JACK MASSA

Jack Massa has published fantasy, science fiction, and magical realist fiction as well as poetry. Past poetry credits include The Lyric, Eccentric Orbits 2, and Bearing Torches, A Devotional Anthology for Hekate. Jack's fiction and blog can be found at triskelionbooks.com.

ALLENE NICHOLS

When not contemplating potential catastrophic futures in her poetry, Allene Nichols writes about travel and home. She also writes poems that re-imagine the lives and loves of famous women in poetry and literature. Her poetry is informed by her experiences teaching English and English teacher's education at The Mississippi University for Women. Her poems have appeared in many journals and anthologies, including Veils, Halos, and Shackles and Impossible Archetype. Most recently, "Eve's Rebellion" appeared in the Minison Project's Sonnet Collection series and her poem "After Writer's Block" appeared in Cardigan Press's Byline Legacies: An Anthology by Writers for Writers.

MICHELLE OUCHAREK-DEO

Writing poetry has been part of Michelle's DNA since she was old enough to pick up a pencil and her love of expressing emotion, or an experience through words guided her throughout her life. Michelle's relationship to poetry, although prolific, has been a private one until now. She looks forward to sharing more of her work in the future. In addition to her poetry Michelle has published two contemporary women's fiction novels and is working on the third in her series.

RK RUGG

RK Rugg is a non-Native native of the American West. A Jewish cowboy now living in New England, he teaches middle-school writing by day and works in SpecFic, SpecNonFic and SpecPo by night. More info at RaymondKRugg.com.

RYFKAH

Transplanted from Chicago to Los Angeles, Ryfkah's poetry has been published extensively in the United States and abroad. The first published poem came about by being awakened from a dream in which God speaks the poem to her and then tells her to get up and go write it down. The first chapbook of her poems was If Venus Had Arms, published by the North Orange County Poetry Continuum. A special honor was being included in Voices, a literary journal in Israel. Her poetry was published in many of the issues of the San Gabriel Poetry Quarterly. Her verse also appeared in such diverse journals as I Love Your Poetry from Palabraproductions and Echoes Rewoven, a poetic dialogue, from HazenStearnsPress. Currently, she is preparing an anthology of poems that focuses on women's voices in the Bible.

JUSTIN SLOANE

Justin's work has appeared in various publications, including The Flying Saucer Poetry Review, The Starlight SciFaiku Review, Southern Cross Review, Sandstorm, The Guardian, The Internet TESL Journal and the Global Ideas Book. In 2002, he was the first winner of the Macmillan Education Onestopenglish poetry contest. Justin is the editor at Starship Sloane Publishing where he has the distinct honor of working with some of the most talented writers and artists in this universe or any other.

JOSHUA ST. CLAIRE

Joshua St. Claire is a certified public accountant who works as a financial controller for a small company. He is a married father of three boys and enjoys writing poetry (often collaborating with his lovely wife) on coffee breaks and after putting his sons to bed. His speculative poetry is published or forthcoming in Star*line, The Flying Saucer Poetry Review, The Starlight Scifaiku Review, The Space Cadet Science Fiction Review, and Scifaikuest, among others, and has received nominations for the Pushcart. He drinks entirely too much coffee and looks forward to replacing his broken espresso machine one day.

SEAN STUBBLEFIELD

Sean Stubblefield is a meta-modern independent author of speculative fiction, poetry, horror, philosophy and media studies. Since 2008, this self-published philosopher-poet has composed over twenty books; available via his website: www.seanstubblefield.com. His current project is a collection of short stories and poetry related to Star Trek during The Four Years War between The Federation and Klingon Empire. Inspired by (and serving as a voluntary unsolicited and unaffiliated companion to) the Star Trek Axanar short film produced by Ares Studios, these stories are posted for free on Medium. Through his writing, Sean aims and attempts-- with varying degrees of success-- to innovate the craft of whatever genre and format he engages. Sean is also involved in media literacy advocacy and social-justice commentary, which can be found on his twitter @wingmanalysis.

REX SWEENY

Rex Sweeny is a poet living in Edinburgh, Scotland. His work has appeared in The Dark Horse, Gutter, Poetry Scotland, The Poets' Republic, The One O'Clock Gun, Dreich, Open Minds Quarterly, As Above So Below and the anthologies New T@les from the Old Town (2013) and Summer Anywhere (2021). In normal times he reads his poems at spoken word events in Edinburgh and East Lothian, including Shore Poets and The Heretics, and organises an annual poetry event for Leith Festival. His favourite poet is Alden Nowlan and he would like his own work to be similarly accessible and moving.

LISA TIMPF

Lisa Timpf's long-time interest in science fiction was sparked by authors like Andre Norton and Robert A. Heinlein, and TV shows like Star Trek: The Original Series. Lisa started writing speculative poetry and short stories of her own in 2014. Since that time, her speculative poetry has appeared in a variety of venues, including Star*Line, Eye to the Telescope, New Myths, Scifaikuest, and Polar Borealis. Lisa's collection of speculative haibun poetry, In Days to Come, is available from Hiraeth Publishing. When not writing, Lisa enjoys bird-watching and organic gardening. Check out lisatimpf.blogspot.com for information about Lisa's writing projects.

LAMONT TURNER

Most of my poems are evocations of fantastical places or unusual states of being, but I have penned some that would be considered social commentary. I have also written a considerable amount of verse for my wife, who is my primary inspiration in life and all creative endeavors. My stories and poems have appeared in numerous print and online venues, including The Stray Branch, Discretionary Love, Tales From The Moonlit Path, Stranger With Friction, and Mystery Magazine. My short story collection, Souls In A Blender, was published by St. Rooster Books in 2021. I can be found on Twitter @LamontATurner1.

WENDY VAN CAMP
Wendy Van Camp is the Poet Laureate for the City of
Anaheim, California. Her work is influenced by cutting edge
technology, astronomy, and daydreams. A graduate of the Ad
Astra Speculative Fiction Workshop, Wendy has won
Honorable Mention at the Writers of the Future Contest, is a
twice nominated finalist for the Elgin Award, and has been
nominated for a Pushcart Prize. Her poems have appeared in:
"Starlight Scifaiku Review", "Quantum Visions", "Eccentric
Orbits", and "Far Horizons". She is the poet and illustrator of
"The Planets: a scifaiku poetry collection".   Find her online at
http://wendyvancamp.com

MIKE VAN HORN
Mike's poems are lyrics of songs sung by his pop-singer
heroine, Selena M. She's the protagonist of his science fiction
stories—Aliens Crashed in My Back Yard, My Spaceship
Calls Out to Me, and Space Girl Yearning. Mike writes stories
with a strong female protagonist, non-hostile aliens, wry
humor, and plausible impossibilities.
His books are at galaxytalltales.com and on Amazon.
He has an MBA from UCLA and lives near San Francisco
with his wife BJ.

RUTH E. WALKER
Ruth E. Walker still has the book she "borrowed" from her
high school library: Ray Bradbury's R is for Rocket. Raised
on fairy tales and fables, her broad literary appetite introduced
her to Shakespeare, Isaac Asimov, Stephen King, and
Margaret Atwood. Poetry taught her how powerful images
stick to the brain. Star Trek (every single series), taught her
how a storyline can be made fresh again and again. Ruth's
poetry has appeared in Science Creative Quarterly, CV2 &
Prairie Fire, among others. She regularly blogs at Writescape
and her fiction is represented by Ali McDonald at 5 Otter
Literary.

TD WALKER
T.D. Walker is the author of the poetry collections Small Waiting Objects (CW Books, 2019) and Maps of a Hollowed World (Another New Calligraphy 2020). Her poems and stories have appeared in Strange Horizons, Web Conjunctions, The Cascadia Subduction Zone, Luna Station Quarterly, and elsewhere. Walker curates and hosts Short Waves / Short Poems, a program created for broadcast on shortwave radio that features poets reading their work. Find out more at https://www.tdwalker.net

LYNN WHITE
Lynn White lives in north Wales. Her work is influenced by issues of social justice and events, places and people she has known or imagined. She is especially interested in exploring the boundaries of dream, fantasy and reality. She was shortlisted in the Theatre Cloud 'War Poetry for Today' competition and has been nominated for a Pushcart Prize, Best of the Net and a Rhysling Award. Her poetry has appeared in many publications including: Apogee, Firewords, Capsule Stories, Gyroscope Review and So It Goes. Find Lynn at: https://lynnwhitepoetry.blogspot.com and https://www.facebook.com/Lynn-White-Poetry-1603675983213077/

JEFF YOUNG

Jeff Young is a bookseller first and a writer second – although he wouldn't mind a reversal of fortune. He is an award winning author who has contributed to the anthologies: Eccentric Orbits Volume 2, Writers of the Future V.26, Afterpunk, In an Iron Cage: The Magic of Steampunk, Clockwork Chaos, Gaslight and Grimm, If We Had Known, Fantastic Futures 13, The Society for the Preservation of C.J. Henderson, TV Gods & TV Gods: Summer Programming, the Defending the Future Military SciFi Anthologies and the forthcoming Beer, Because Your Friends Aren't That Interesting. Jeff's own fiction is collected in Spirit Seeker and TOI Special Edition 2 – Diversiforms. He has also edited the Drunken Comic Book Monkey line, TV Gods and TV Gods – Summer Programming and has joined the Novels Guys as part of Fortress Publishing, Inc. He has led the Watch the Skies SF&F Discussion Group of Camp Hill and Harrisburg for nineteen years. http://www.jy.watchtheskies.org